Farmed Out

Christy Goerzen

Orca currents

ORCA BOOK PUBLISHERS

Library and Archives Canada Cataloguing in Publication

Goerzen, Christy, 1975-
Farmed out / Christy Goerzen.
(Orca currents)

Issued also in electronic format.
ISBN 978-1-55469-911-7 (bound).--ISBN 978-1-55469-910-0 (pbk.)

I. Title. II. Series: Orca currents
PS8613.O38F37 2011   JC813'.6   C2011-903349-6

First published in the United States, 2011
Library of Congress Control Number: 2011929396

Summary: Fifteen-year-old Maddie, an artist with big-city dreams, is forced to volunteer on an organic farm.

Orca Book Publishers is dedicated to preserving the environment and has printed this book on paper certified by the Forest Stewardship Council®.

Orca Book Publishers gratefully acknowledges the support for its publishing programs provided by the following agencies: the Government of Canada through the Canada Book Fund and the Canada Council for the Arts, and the Province of British Columbia through the BC Arts Council and the Book Publishing Tax Credit.

Cover photography by iStockphoto.com

ORCA BOOK PUBLISHERS
PO Box 5626, Stn. B
Victoria, BC Canada
V8R 6S4

ORCA BOOK PUBLISHERS
PO Box 468
Custer, WA USA
98240-0468

www.orcabook.com
Printed and bound in Canada.

14 13 12 11 • 4 3 2 1

For Tara, with buckets of love

Chapter One

"Okay, Maddie, let's talk adventure."

I groaned across the kitchen table at my mother. I thought we could avoid the "adventure" topic that summer. Silly me.

For the past few years my mom has made me go on summer "adventures." Whoever taught her the definition of that word obviously didn't understand English very well.

Last July is a prime example. She dragged me to a Wild Woman Weekend on Saltspring Island. It was at this hippie lady's house. I think her name was Star Mountain Skyhawk. She had stringy gray hair down to her butt, and stringy gray armpit hair to match. Gross. The basic gist of the weekend was that we paint on our faces with mud and scream into a hole in the ground. Then we all sat in a circle and talked about our womanly feelings. It was me, my mom and a bunch of middle-aged women, like always.

Our summer adventures are my mother's big chance to express what she calls her "true self." My mom is a book-keeper, which is like an accountant that doesn't make much money. She wears beige pantyhose and high heels every day. Outside of work, she's totally New Age. She even has a side business as a tarot card reader. A corner of our living room is draped with velvet scarves and crystals for her clients. Most of them are desperate single women looking for true love.

But I hoped that this summer adventure would be different. Maybe this year we'd go to New York City and visit art galleries. Art is my thing, and New York is the place to see lots of it. But that was a crazy idea. A silly fantasy. My mother would never in a million years have an idea as cool as going to New York City.

I had my own plans for getting to the Big Apple anyway. My favorite art magazine, *Canvas*, was running a youth art contest. And the prize was…drum roll, please: a one-week, all-expenses-paid trip to New York City. This included passes to all the art galleries in town. *And* the winning piece would appear on the cover of the magazine. In other words, a huge deal.

It was the chance of a lifetime. The entry deadline was in eight days. I hadn't started drawing, but I do my best work at the last minute. I planned to hang out downtown at the art gallery for inspiration.

"Um...adventure?" I asked, my fingers and toes crossed under the table.

With a flourish, my mom held up a green booklet.

I squinted to read the cover.

My mom set down her coffee mug and stood up as though she was about to give an Oscar acceptance speech.

"We are going to experience the rewards of organic farming."

Visions of me sketching in a Manhattan café vanished instantly. *Wishful thinking, Maddie.* My mom couldn't afford to take us anywhere exciting.

Mom had a huge grin on her face as she sat back down. She always gets worked up about our mother-daughter trips.

"Organic farming?"

Mom slid the booklet across the table saying, "We'll be VOF-ers! That's what the volunteers are called."

VOFO, the cover read. *Volunteer Organic Farm Opportunities*. A bunch of the pages were dog-eared.

I flipped through the booklet. Paragraphs about farms all over the province were circled in yellow highlighter. There were farms on Vancouver Island, in Powell River, the Okanagan and Nelson.

"Go to the Central Okanagan section," she said, "and read about the farm in Mara."

I started to read the description to myself.

"Read it out loud," she said, her eyes shiny.

I sighed. All I wanted to do was eat a bowl of junky cereal and watch TV.

"*Quiet River Farm*," I read. "*Proprietors: Klaus and Ruth Friesen. Come join us on our fifty-acre patch of paradise. We have a dairy cow, goats, pigs, chickens and a garlic garden. Work varies from animal care to weeding. If you love country living and good food, please come stay with us.*"

"Doesn't it sound *perfect*?" My mom clapped her hands together. "I've always wanted to learn about living off the land."

"Since when?"

I flipped through the rest of the book. *Come build a sweat lodge with us,* said a farmer from Nelson. *You'll enjoy our organic fertilizer operation*, said a guy named John van Horne in Kaslo. There were cheesemakers, herb farmers and even sheepherders.

"We only have to work for four hours a day," my mom said. She took a gulp from her coffee mug. "We'll learn so much, us urban gals."

Having to work "only" four hours a day didn't make this trip sound better. I crossed my arms and gave her the classic Maddie Turner stare.

"Mom, these people are complete nutbars."

My mom stopped smiling. She raked her fingers through her long blond hair. It's not her natural color. She bleaches it.

"Maddie," my mom continued, her voice raspy. It gets like that when she's annoyed. "You've never felt earth between your fingers. You've never known what it's like to till the soil with your own two hands."

"Don't they have machines for that?" I said.

"You were born and raised in the city. Your high school is in downtown Vancouver. We live in a tenth-floor apartment." Mom plucked a couple of mint leaves from the clay pot on the table and held them up. "This is the closest we get to nature. Every fifteen-year-old girl should get in touch with the earth."

"No," I said, slapping my hand on the table. "Fifteen-year-old girls should spend the summer sleeping in and hanging out with their friends as far away from manure as possible."

"Come on, Maddie, it'll be good for both of us to get out of the city for a week."

"A week!"

"We leave Saturday morning."

"Saturday morning!" I spluttered. "In, like, two days? But what about the *Canvas* art contest? The deadline is eight days away!"

Another thing about our adventures is that my mom never gives me any notice—or asks my opinion. She says she likes to "maintain the element of surprise."

"You could do it before we leave."

"I can't! I'm babysitting all day tomorrow!" I could feel my face tense with frustration.

"Well, honey, maybe you'll find inspiration on the farm. A lot of great artists lived in the country. Bring your art stuff along with you."

"I can't get inspiration on a stupid farm! I can't believe you're doing this to me!" My eyes were hot with tears. My mom was going to ruin *everything*.

"Madison, calm down. Deep breath." My mom put her index fingers

9

and thumbs together, yoga-style, and inhaled loudly through her nose. "It'll all work out."

I crossed my arms and kicked the table leg with my toe.

"Honey, this will be fun," my mom said, her hands still in the yoga position.

"Can I go stay with Dad?" I said, interrupting her. I said that just to make her mad. My mom looked like she might cry.

"No you may *not*. This is our mother-daughter trip." She stomped into the living room and turned on the TV.

"You're mad?" I called after her. "I'm the one watching all my hopes and dreams crumble!"

Like all of our mother-daughter adventures, I didn't have a choice. I was going to Quiet River Farm whether I liked it or not.

By Friday night I still hadn't packed.
I sat on my bed and looked at myself in
my dresser mirror. I had just cropped my
blond hair short and added bright blue
streaks. I wondered what the farmers
would think of my hair.

I yanked open my dresser drawer and
started throwing all my most fabulous
clothes into a duffel bag. *You can take
the girl out of the city,* I thought, *but you
can't take the city out of the girl.* I wasn't
planning to pack the ratty old T-shirts and
jeans my mom wanted me to wear.

I plucked my sketchbook off my
desk and sat on my bed, flipping
through it. My latest series, *Downtown
Soles*, had turned out pretty well. I had
drawn feet in cool shoes at different
city locations like the art gallery and the
skate park.

As I carefully placed my art supplies
inside the bag, I felt a new flush
of frustration. What was the point?

I would never, ever find anything to draw on a boring old farm.

My mom walked by my bedroom door. "How's it going, Madison?" She had consulted her tarot cards and decided to forgive me for our fight the day before.

I was still nowhere near forgiving *her*.

"If you mean how's it going with missing out on the chance of a lifetime, then just *fine*."

My mom started rifling through the stuff I had packed. Mothers can be so nosy.

"Maddie, these aren't exactly work clothes." She held up my yellow crinoline and striped leggings. "We're going to be getting dirty. You don't want to ruin these."

I threw my pink *What Would Joan Jett Do?* T-shirt in the bag. I knew what that 1970s rocker chick would do.

She would *not* spend a week shoveling cow poop.

I tossed my cell phone charger on top of the T-shirt. Mom laughed.

"You might as well leave that at home," she said. "No cell phone reception at Quiet River Farm."

No cell phone? This was going to be the worst week *ever*.

Chapter Two

"Hurry up, sunshine. Chop chop!"

My mom always says "chop chop" to get me to hurry. This makes me want to throw something heavy at her. My Betty Boop alarm clock said *5:45 AM*. Was she kidding? After she told me to chop chop a dozen more times, I hauled myself out of bed.

I stumbled through the beaded curtain into the kitchen. Our apartment's decor is a lot like my mom—an odd mix of office slave and goddess worshipper. In other words, tacky, tacky, tacky.

My mom sat at the table, packing apples and bottles of water into a cooler. She stood up as soon as I walked in.

"What do you think?" She did a little twirl. She was wearing a plaid shirt with the sleeves rolled up, denim overalls that were three sizes too big, a straw hat and black rubber boots. It looked like a Halloween farmer costume.

"Where's the piece of hay to stick between your teeth?" I said.

"Right here." She stuck a long piece of grass between her teeth. "I got it from the park yesterday."

"That probably has dog pee all over it," I groaned and yanked the fridge door open.

Inside was half a tomato, a nearly empty jar of mustard and a carton of blueberry yogurt. Sometimes my mom gets so into living spiritually that she forgets to buy groceries.

"Just think," my mom said, the grass still sticking out of her mouth. "In less than seven hours we'll be petting goats!"

My mom blabbed in a nonstop monologue the whole car ride. She was trying to make up for my lack of interest by being enthusiastic for both of us.

I crossed my arms and looked out the window the whole time. She still didn't understand how angry I was.

"I really want to learn more about organic cooking. Ooh, I wonder if we'll get to milk a goat. That would be fun. Maybe we'll feed the chickens and pigs!"

After about five torturous hours, our ancient 1984 Dodge Colt started overheating. I couldn't believe it had gotten us that far.

"Dave needs a rest," Mom said as we pulled off the highway. She calls her car Dave, after an old boyfriend. "Perfect! I've heard they have the best veggie burgers at The Hut here."

Vegetarianism was my mom's latest thing. She had even stuck a bumper sticker on the car that said, *Animals are my friends. I don't eat my friends.*

We pulled into the parking lot of the A-frame burger joint. I sat at a picnic table outside while my mom ordered.

"Here's your poor dead cow," my mom said, plopping burgers and fries on the picnic table. Just because my mom was a vegetarian didn't mean I had to be.

"This whole thing is like a lame sitcom," I said, sipping my chocolate milkshake. "City girl goes to the country. City girl hates the country.

It's a tired old storyline. Couldn't we do something more original?"

My mom poured disgusting amounts of vinegar over her fries. "Sometimes the city girl ends up *loving* the country."

I snorted. *That* was doubtful. I decided to focus on my burger. It was a tasty chunk of dead cow.

After pouring three pop bottles' worth of water into Dave's radiator, we chugged into the countryside. Everything was lush and green. It brought to mind a word we learned in English class—*verdant*. It described this place perfectly.

We drove past fields with rows and rows of green vegetables. In one of the fields, an oversized lawn sprinkler was spraying a thick brown liquid. Just as I was wondering what it was, the smell hit me.

"Aaaagh!" my mom and I screamed in unison, plugging our noses. We rolled up our windows. It didn't help. Wow, I thought. That was a giant poo sprinkler.

Eventually we turned down a winding dirt road. My mom's rattly old car clanged over railway tracks.

"Here we are," my mom sang.

The handmade wooden sign at the end of the driveway said *Quiet River Farm*. What a perfect name for a place that looked like a total snooze fest.

Our hosts were on their front porch in matching rocking chairs. They stood up as Dave coasted to a stop, crashing into a big pot of orange flowers. Chickens squawked and scattered, feathers flying.

"Oh no, I freaked the animals!" my mom said.

Dave jerked and backfired. I sank down in my seat, my cheeks burning. Not only was my mother ruining my life, she was also going to totally embarrass me in the process.

Mom flung the car door open and leaped out.

"I'm sorry about your flowers," my mom said, running up to the farmers. Her voice was shaky. "I'm Lynn Turner, and this is my daughter, Maddie." She hugged them. My mom gets touchy-feely when she's nervous.

"Welcome here," the man farmer said, taking a couple of steps back. He had a German accent, or maybe it was Dutch. I wasn't up on my European accents. "I'm Klaus Friesen, and this is my wife, Ruth."

A big yellow dog poked my leg with his black nose. It tickled.

"And this is Harold the dog," Ruth said.

The Friesens gave my mom and me a long look up and down, starting with the blue streaks in my hair. My mom, of course, still wore her farmer costume. I was wearing fishnet tights, a black ruffled skirt and my Andy Warhol soup can T-shirt.

"Good to see you have your work boots on," Klaus said, pointing to my Doc Martens. If he thought I was going to work in my prized boots, he was crazy.

The Friesens looked like they were in their early fifties. I had expected hippie types, but hippies they definitely were not. Klaus was tall, and was wearing overalls and a Buckerfield's Feed & Grain trucker cap. He had the biggest hands I have ever seen. Ruth's hair was half brown, half gray, and pulled back in a loose bun. She wore a long jean skirt and an old-fashioned blouse with little blue flowers all over it. They looked like they were out of an old painti

"We feel so blessed t
in your amazing space,"

blathered on. I half-expected her to put her hands in the prayer position, bow and say "namaste."

The Friesens stared blankly at my mom. Klaus took off his cap and scratched his head.

At that moment I knew which painting they reminded me of. It's a famous one of a skinny older man and woman, standing in front of a barn. It's a creepy painting. *American Gothic*, it's called.

"Yeesh," I muttered under my breath, shuddering.

"What was that, Maddie?" my mom asked.

"Nothing," I said.

Chapter Three

"Anna will be excited to meet you," Ruth said, passing me a jar of home-made plum jam.

We were having a "bite" in the farm-house kitchen. The Friesens' idea of a bite was an all-you-can-eat deluxe spread. I'd never seen anything like it. Their huge table was covered in pitchers of milk and juice, loaves of bread and buns, jars of jam and honey, a bowl of hard-boiled eggs, and plates of cheese, meat, tomatoes and pickles. I had loaded up my plate and was about to dig into a bun filled with Swiss cheese and ham.

"Anna?" my mom and I said in unison.

"Our daughter," Ruth said. "She's about your age, Maddie. Fifteen."

"She's at a meeting right now," Klaus said. "The summer fair is coming up."

Fifteen. The same age as me. Thoughts flew around in my mind. What did Anna look like? Would we get along?

"That's great that Maddie will have someone her own age here," my mom said, cracking open a hard-boiled egg. Usually on our adventures there were never any other kids around, just adults. Ha, I thought. Not this time, Mom.

Klaus offered my mom a plate of sausages.

"Oh, no thank you," said my mom. "I'm a vegetarian."

Ruth and Klaus exchanged looks. I thought I saw Klaus roll his eyes. I took the plate from Klaus and helped myself to four sausages. They looked delicious.

It didn't take my mom long to launch into dumb-question mode.

"Why did you become farmers? When do you harvest your wheat? How many chickens do you have?"

Klaus said something about being a fifth-generation farmer. I tuned out the rest. Farming wasn't the most exciting topic.

While my mom grilled the farmers, I looked around. The house looked about a hundred years old. The walls were white, with plain yellow curtains on the windows. The only picture on the wall was an old black-and-white family photo where no one was smiling.

I couldn't see a TV or computer anywhere.

"Do you wake up every day and notice the smell of manure, or do you become immune to it after a while?" Mom asked.

I sank down in my chair. Ruth and Klaus smiled. My mom kept yakking.

After we ate, the Friesens showed us to our room. A four-poster iron bed stood in the center of the room, covered in a colorful quilt. Great. Sharing a bed with my mother made a bad situation even worse.

"Oooh!" my mom exclaimed, clapping her hands as she looked around the room. "Very *Little House on the Prairie*. And look, Maddie, we get to share a bed. It'll be like a sleepover!"

Shut up, Mom, I thought for the hundredth time that day. I wasn't sure I could handle a whole week of constant embarrassment. Hopefully I could find somewhere to hide out and draw for the *Canvas* art contest.

After showing us our room, Ruth and Klaus led us out to the front yard to give us the "grand tour." Just then, a teenage girl turned into the driveway on a red bike.

"Here's our girl," Klaus said. The girl skidded neatly to a stop, a small cloud of dust billowing from beneath her back tire. "Anna, these are our volunteers for the next week, Lynn and Maddie Turner."

"Hey," Anna said with a small smile. She had braces and wore her red hair in a long braid.

"How was the 4-H meeting?" Ruth asked.

Anna shrugged. "Pretty good."

"I just checked Frida," Klaus said. "I'm certain that she will calve in the next few days."

Anna nodded and turned to us. "I've got a cow that's about to pop."

I wondered how many other farm volunteers Anna had had to greet so far that summer. She didn't seem too excited by us.

"You and Maddie are the same age, dear," Klaus said. "Maybe you two would like to spend some time together."

"Yeah, maybe," Anna said, not looking in my direction. "If I have time." She turned on her heel and clumped up the stairs in her muddy work boots.

Adults saying, "Hey kids, why don't you two play," is exactly what will prevent teenage girls from getting to know each other. I didn't blame Anna for leaving.

Next on the farm tour was the pigpen. It was the width of two cars, with solid wood walls all around it.

My mom and I peered over the wall at the big mama pig laying on her side with her piglets jostling to get some milk.

"Look at that poor runt," my mom said. "The other piglets are squishing him."

"Such is the life of a runt," Ruth said. "Often they don't survive."

My mom looked like she might cry. She'd probably try to sneak the runt home with us as a pet.

Ruth and Klaus showed us the vegetable garden, the garlic field, the machine shed and the barn. A clear, slow-moving river ran along one side of the farm, near the road, and a tree-covered mountain rose up behind the farmhouse.

My mom asked inane questions the entire tour.

"Do pigs really eat slops? Is it hard to milk a cow? Do you use a horse and plow?"

The Friesens took turns patiently responding to my mom's questions. Yes, Klaus said, the pigs liked apple peels and table scraps. No, Ruth replied, it just takes a little practice to get the milk out. No, Klaus said, he used his tractors to till the fields.

In the afternoon heat, the farm smell was everything I'd expected, and more. It was a combination of various types of animal poop, hay, dirt and something else even more powerful.

"What's that smell?" my mom asked, plugging her nose and squeezing her eyes shut.

Ruth chuckled. She pointed past the vegetable garden. "The goats."

"That's your first job," Klaus said.

Chapter Four

We were outside the goat shed, standing in three inches of stinky mud. About twenty goats surrounded us, bleating and chewing. I had never seen a goat in real life before. They had creepy eyes with long narrow pupils.

"What are all their names?" my mom asked. My mother named everything, from her hair dryer (Barbara) to her car

(Dave, of course). Her favorite high heels were named Mary and Rhoda.

"They don't have names," Ruth said.

"We don't like to get too attached," Klaus said. "They are our business, not pets."

Klaus handed each of us a shovel. "First you will muck out the shed."

What kind of torture chamber was this place? Mucking out a goat shed?

"You do it like so," he said, skimming his shovel over the floor to scoop up hard round goat poops. "Then, you dump it over the side for composting later." He turned the shovel over and tapped it on the open side of the shed. The little poops plopped into a pile.

I looked down at my beloved Andy Warhol T-shirt. It already had a streak of mud on it.

Then I felt a tug on my skirt. A brown and white goat had a mouthful of black ruffles.

"Ack, no!" I exclaimed, trying to pry the skirt out of its mouth. I got it out, but a big chunk had ripped off. The goat scampered away, spraying muck all over my legs.

"I told you not to bring those clothes," my mom said, in that way mothers are so good at.

"You can borrow something of Anna's, if you don't have anything suitable," Ruth said.

I didn't want to wear farm-girl clothes, but I didn't want mine to get all ripped and stained either.

"Okay," I said. "Thanks."

Five minutes later I was decked out in one of Anna's T-shirts and light blue jeans. I felt like such a dork.

When I returned to the goat shed, my mom was shoveling poop and singing "Old MacDonald Had a Farm" to herself. She changed the words to "Young Lynn Turner Had a Farm."

I decided to take out my anger by shoveling. I dreamed of being back in the city, sitting in my favorite café with my sketchbook.

"Isn't this fun, Maddie?" my mom said. "Hard work builds character."

I didn't respond. I shoveled harder, trying to drown out whatever other clichés were coming out of her mouth.

A few minutes later my mom leaned her shovel against the shed wall. She raised her arms and did a big stretch. "Well, this has been fun. I wonder what we get to do next."

I straightened up. "What are you talking about? We're supposed to clean the whole shed."

"Oh. Right," my mom said, looking disappointed.

If my mom was going to not like the farm work, then I was going to *love* it.

I continued to muck out the shed, whistling as I worked.

My mom said something, but I pretended not to hear her over the sound of my vigorous scooping.

I was getting into a rhythm. *Scoop poop, poop scoop*, I repeated in my head.

I wasn't sure how much time had gone by, but when I looked up again, my mom was gone.

"Mom?" I called. I poked my head around the side of the shed.

There she was, with a small herd of goats nibbling at her sleeves and nuzzling her knees. She stroked a brown goat's floppy ears. She was holding something in her right hand. Two of the goats had words written on them.

"Mom, what are you doing?"

She looked up, her hand poised over the left butt cheek of a white goat.

I realized the thing in her hand was a muddy stick.

"Oh hi, Madison," she said, as though using dirt to scribble on farm animals was normal. "Come see. I'm naming the goats."

The white goat scurried away. It had *Glenda* printed in big muddy letters on its flank. The butt of another goat victim said *Gigi*.

"Mom, have you gone completely nuts?" I said finally, tossing down my shovel. The goats scattered.

"Not at all," she replied, her chin held high. "I'm writing their names on the goats so that the Friesens can remember who they are."

"Well, stop it right now!" I yelled.

Ruth and Klaus approached, carrying armfuls of hay. I covered my face with my hands in pure embarrassment. Oh *no*.

"Good gracious!" Ruth exclaimed when she saw the goats.

"Meet Glenda and Gigi," my mom said. "And there's Grace, Geena, Giselle and Ginger, but I haven't gotten to them yet. I thought I would start a tradition of naming your farm animals," she added proudly.

I sucked in a breath, waiting to see what the Friesens would say. Klaus slowly took his pipe out of his breast pocket, lit it and took a puff.

"Gigi and Glenda are heading to the slaughterhouse tomorrow," he said. "We supply restaurants with goat meat."

My mom's eyes went pink and teary. "Gigi and Glenda?" she said, her voice weak. "That's what these goats are destined for? Certain *death*?"

I understood why the Friesens didn't name their animals.

"Why don't you take a break and come in for some iced tea," Ruth said.

"Okay," my mom said. She dropped the muddy stick.

"I'm going to go for a walk," I said. "But I'll come in soon."

I wanted to wander around the farm and get inspired for the art contest. I thought it was doubtful I'd find something to draw, but I might as well stay away from my mother for a while.

I walked past the tractors and the vegetable garden. It amazed me how they got those long lines of vegetables so perfectly straight. Past the garden was the barn. The door was wide open in the late afternoon sun. It was one of those classic red barns with white trim, like what you see in children's books.

Anna sat inside on a wooden stool, oiling some leather straps. Behind her was an enormously pregnant brown cow. Her sides stuck out so much that she barely fit in her stall.

"Hi," I said from the doorway.

"Hey," Anna said, not looking up.

Above the cow's stall was a hand-painted nameplate that read *Frida Cowlo*.

"Your cow's name is Frida Cowlo?"

Anna nodded, still not looking up.

"After Frida Kahlo, the Mexican painter?" I continued.

"Yeah." Anna paused and looked at me with narrowed eyes. Then she turned back to her work.

I couldn't hide my enthusiasm. "Cool! She's one of my favorite artists."

Anna sighed and set down the leather straps. "Is there something you wanted?" She looked up again. "Why are you wearing my clothes?"

Oh crap. I had forgotten about that. My time at Quiet River Farm so far was a string of embarrassing moments. "Uh, your mom lent them to me," I said. "For working in."

I tried to fix the situation by acting like it was no big deal. "So, what are you doing?"

"Look, I'm very busy here." She turned away.

It appeared that Anna hated me. With her freckles and round blue eyes, she looked like she'd be nice.

"I just came to say hi." I paused. No response. "Okay, bye." I slouched out of the barn.

My mom was a weirdo, I was wearing a 4-H Cow Club T-shirt, and the one person my age in this boring place hated me. At least the food was good. But I still wondered what I had done to deserve this.

Chapter Five

The next morning a rooster woke me up. Seriously. Just like in cartoons. It even made a *cock-a-doodle-doo* sound.

"Make it stop," my mom groaned and turned over, pulling her pillow around her ears.

There was a sharp knock on our door. "Bacon's on!" Klaus bellowed.

Remembering the spread the day before, I rolled myself out of bed. I couldn't wait to see what breakfast would be.

"Mom? You coming?" No answer. She didn't eat bacon anyway. I prodded her a few times, but she kept saying, "Five more minutes, five more minutes!" Let sleeping mothers lie, I thought.

The smells of fresh coffee and bread rushed into my nose as soon as I entered the kitchen.

"Good morning!" Ruth and Klaus said.

The table was laden with food—canned peaches, bread, butter, cheese, eggs, jam and orange juice. Had I died and gone to Breakfast Heaven? This sure beat the stale cereal and almost-expired milk I usually ate.

I looked at the clock above the sink. Six o'clock. Farmers sure did get up early.

"Is your mother coming?" Klaus asked.

"Yeah, I think she'll wake up soon."

The three of us sat down and started filling our plates. Half an hour passed with no sign of my mom. I didn't mind so much. It was nice and quiet without her.

"Is Anna here?" I asked.

"She's been in the barn since five," Ruth said. Anna was starting to make me feel like a lazy kid.

After breakfast I walked along the edge of the garlic field, thinking about the *Canvas* art contest. I had my sketchbook and pencils with me in case I got inspired. Time was running out.

It was misty and fresh and perfectly farmlike. Everything was completely still. The only sound was that rooster, still crowing somewhere in the distance.

I plunked myself down on a patch of yellowed grass and opened my sketchbook. I had taped the ad for the art contest to the inside cover. I read it for the hundredth time.

The First Annual "Face of Youth" Art Contest—for artists ages 13–17. Think you've got what it takes? This year's theme is Portraits. Send us your best drawing, painting or mixed media piece of an interesting face, and you could win an all-expenses-paid trip to New York City. First prize includes an all-access pass to the city's art galleries. The winner will be featured on the cover of Canvas Magazine. *Entries must be postmarked by July 25.*

I got a rush of adrenaline. July 25 was now only five days away. I had to think of the most fabulous drawing ever. And fast.

Harold the dog ran up and poked his wet nose into my armpit. I giggled. He lay down and wiggled around on his back for a belly rub.

"Oh yes, Harold, what a good boy!" I said, rubbing his stomach. I'm more of a cat person, but Harold seemed sweet. He soon settled into a regal pose beside me, surveying the farm. I decided that Harold was as good a subject as any, and picked up my pencil.

After a few minutes I felt someone watching me. Anna was leaning against the barn, looking at me with her chin lifted.

I turned back to my sketchbook. I heard Anna's footsteps as she clumped over to me.

"What're you doing?" she asked, standing over me.

"Drawing Harold," I said.

She peered at the drawing. So far I had sketched his floppy ears and the top of his head.

"Looks pretty good." She sat down and started petting Harold. "Harold's an excellent judge of character. He only likes good people."

I wasn't sure what to do. Keep sketching, or stop? I continued to sketch.

"So you're from Vancouver?" Anna said after a while.

"Um-hmm," I answered. By then I had drawn most of Harold's face.

Silence. When I was working on Harold's collar, Anna spoke again.

"We don't get a lot of volunteers from Vancouver," she said. "Mostly we get hippie types from Nelson looking for an 'experience.'" She made air quotes with her fingers when she said "experience."

"That's what my mom is here for," I said. "Except she calls it an 'adventure.'" I made air quotes.

Anna laughed. Her laugh was hard, like it was coming out of a forty-year-old woman who smokes a lot.

"I can't stand hippies," Anna said matter-of-factly.

"Yeah, my mom is really into the DDP factor when it comes to our adventures," I said.

"DDP?" Anna asked.

"Drums, dreadlocks and patchouli."

Anna's eyes widened. "DDP! That totally describes the volunteers."

"One time my mom took me to a drum circle at the beach," I said, "and some guy wouldn't let us sit on this log because the spirit of Jimi Hendrix was already sitting on it."

Anna laughed again even harder. "Was he like, 'Dude, that's Jimi's log'?"

She had the slow, drawling voice of a hippie down perfectly.

Pretty soon we were both rolling around on the grass, killing ourselves laughing over hippie jokes.

"My dad told me that your mom named the goats," Anna said. "He had a heck of a time scrubbing that dirt off."

"Yeah, can you believe it?" I said. "I'm worried about what else she might do."

"Do you want to go swimming in the river?" Anna asked.

"I'd love to." I didn't bring my vintage polka-dot bikini for nothing.

Chapter Six

The river water was clear and cool, and it tugged us along with gentle insistence.

"Wow," I said, dragging my toes along the silky sand of the riverbed. "I've never swum in anything but a chlorine-filled pool."

Anna stuck out her tongue. "Ew, those are full of little-kid pee."

She ducked her head under the water and did a front somersault.

As Anna and I splashed around, I looked out at the farm. The goats were eating their breakfast of cornhusks. The chickens were pecking at their grain. Frida the cow was hanging out beside the barn, basking in the morning sun.

And there was my mother in a bright pink unitard.

"Oh no," I groaned. Not again.

"Maddie?" Anna said.

Not taking my eyes off my mom, who was standing beside the pigpen, I said, "Look over there."

My mom started waving her arms around in big circles, leaning over the pigpen fence. I could hear her chanting "Om." I wondered what the mother pig and her newborn piglets were thinking.

My mom leaned over farther, her arms making wild circles in front of her.

"What is she doing?" Anna asked.

All of a sudden my mom's flip-flop-clad feet flew up in the air. And then everything was still.

I can't remember what I said, but it made Anna gasp. We swam to shore and raced toward the pigpen.

Through the wooden boards, I saw my mother laying in several inches of mud. Six hungry piglets were shoving their snouts into her side. They pulled at her unitard, their tiny mouths full of bright pink spandex.

"Ow! Ow!" my mom yelped. Squirming around in the mud, she tried to sit up, but the piglets had her pinned. "Girls! Help me!"

A piglet ran over her forehead, leaving mud streaks down the side of her face.

I was about to jump in and help my mom when I noticed the mama pig on the other side of the pigpen. She was behind a small wooden gate, squealing like crazy and stamping her hooves. She sounded like a dentist's drill on turbo speed. The mama pig was butting her head against the flimsy gate, trying to get to her piglets.

I seriously started fearing for my mom's life. "Look, look!" I squealed to Anna, almost as loud as the pig.

"Oh no, that pig's about to blow!" Anna said.

It took two seconds for Anna to hop over the fence and yank my mom up by the wrists. They stumbled out of the pigpen with the sow chasing madly after them. Still squealing, the mama pig slammed into the fence.

Anna landed hard on the grass, and my mom fell on top of her with a loud "oof."

"Are you okay?" I said, rushing over to kneel beside them. Anna nodded and jumped up. We stood over my mom, who was moaning something about swine karma.

Klaus and Ruth must have heard the commotion, because they rushed outside.

On the Friesens' faces I saw the true meaning of the word *stunned*. They looked from Anna and me to my mud-covered, unitard-wearing mom laying on the ground, and back again.

Trembling, my mom stood up. I put a hand on her shoulder to steady her. Chunks of hay were stuck to her face and hair. Her mud-caked unitard was full of little holes.

"I-I...," my mom started to say. She paused to spit dirt out of her mouth. "I was just trying to give the piglets some healing vibes. I didn't think they'd try to *suckle* me like that."

"Healing vibes?" Klaus asked. With his German accent, it sounded like "wibes."

My mom straightened up and took a deep breath. She was trying to hold on to a tiny scrap of dignity. "Yes. I just took Level Two Reiki."

"Reiki?" Ruth asked, looking at my mom like she was speaking alien.

Anna couldn't hold it in. She started with a spitty sort of chuckle, but soon she was laughing so hard that she fell back on the grass, her mouth open in a silent howl.

Klaus and Ruth were much more polite. Solemnly, Ruth took my mom by both hands.

"Come, dear," she said, as though my mom were a child. "Let's get you cleaned up."

"Okay," my mom said weakly.

"Why don't you work in the garlic shed from now on," Ruth added.

I turned away and bit my lip to keep from laughing. It was only day two, and my mom was already out of control.

Chapter Seven

I knocked on Anna's bedroom door at 5:00 AM the next day, fuzzy-eyed and still wearing my pajamas. I wanted to catch her before she went out to the barn.

Getting up had almost killed me. I had set the alarm for 4:30 AM and had smacked the snooze button over and over again. My mom slept through the whole thing. How the heck did Anna get up so early every day?

"Who is it?" Anna said through the closed door.

"It's Maddie," I croaked.

Anna opened the door. She wore jean shorts and a red T-shirt, and her hair was braided again. I wondered how long she'd been awake.

"Whoa, you're up early," Anna said.

"Can I borrow some clothes again?"

"Did you only bring city clothes?" Anna said.

I felt my face turn pink. "Uh, well—"

"I'm kidding," Anna said, grinning. "Come in."

She opened a drawer and rummaged through it. Beside the dresser was a shelf with trophies and medals on it, along with photos of Anna wearing medals and standing next to her cow.

Anna tossed me a T-shirt and jeans.

I unfolded the navy blue shirt. I couldn't believe what I was seeing. "This is a Columbia University T-shirt!"

"Yeah, so?"

"Columbia is in New York City!" I squeaked.

"My older brother Thomas is there on a math scholarship." She pointed to a computer in the corner of her room. The desktop photo was of her and a tall, dark-haired guy at a beach.

"I know, ancient, right?" Anna said, turning to look at her computer. "And we only have dial-up. But it does the trick—"

"Have you *been* there?" I interrupted. I could feel my eyes bulging with excitement. I must have looked crazy.

"No," Anna shook her head. "But my parents have."

I tried to imagine Ruth and Klaus in the Big Apple, among all the taxis, crowds and skyscrapers.

"I really want to go though. I've been saving up," Anna said.

This was so surreal. I was talking about New York City with a farmer's daughter at five o'clock in the morning.

"Hang on," I said. "I'll be right back."

I crept into the room where my mom was snoring away and grabbed my sketchbook. I ran back into Anna's room and opened it to the ad for the *Canvas* art contest.

"I figure this is my ticket to New York," I said. "I've wanted to go there forever, to see all the art galleries."

Anna read the ad. "Cool," she said. "So, a portrait? What are you entering?"

"I haven't actually started anything yet."

Anna raised her eyebrows. "Isn't the deadline in a few days?"

"Yeah, I know," I said sheepishly. "I'm a procrastinator. I do my best work at the last minute."

"Are you going to draw someone here? On our farm?" Anna seemed unsure that the farm offered someone worthy of winning the contest.

"Wait, I just got an idea," I said, trying to keep from laughing. I closed my eyes, put my arms out in front of me and started making circles with my hands.

"Imagine me in a pink unitard. Ommmmm…" I chanted.

Anna giggled, covering her mouth with her hand. I laughed way too loud.

"Sssshhhh," Anna said. "The Reiki master has to rest her healing wibes." She imitated Klaus's accent.

It was too much. We collapsed on Anna's bed, trying to laugh quietly, which only made us laugh more.

"It's my turn to deal with the chickens," Anna said after a few minutes of wheezy giggling. "Want to come?"

"What do we have to do?"

"Get the eggs. It's cool. No poop involved."

Anna had read my mind. I'd had enough of animal droppings for the time being. Forever, actually.

After a gigantic breakfast of French toast, hash browns and sausages, Anna and I headed over to the chicken coop. My mom was still sleeping. Ruth said that she would set her to work trimming and scrubbing garlic when she woke up. I think Ruth wanted to keep my mother far away from the animals.

"Good morning, my little hens," Anna whispered, clicking open the wooden half-door to the coop.

The chicken coop was warm and dim. As my eyes adjusted to the dark, I could see a ledge lined with cubbyholes.

Each cubby had a sleeping chicken inside. With their reddish feathers rising and falling on their puffed-out chests, they looked cozy.

"The key is to get the eggs while they're sleeping," Anna said. "Watch."

Very slowly, Anna reached her hand under a chicken. After a few seconds she pulled it out with a brown egg in her palm. The hen didn't even stir. Anna placed the egg in the basket she'd brought.

"Okay, now you try," she said.

"Will they wake up and peck my eyes out?" Obviously I'd watched way too many horror movies.

"No. Now go." Anna raised my hand to the level of the next cubby.

Just like Anna had, I reached my fingers under the chicken. I could feel the warm soft weight of its feathery body, and the egg underneath it. I folded my fingers around the egg and carefully pulled it out.

I stared at the egg. Wow, I'd done it!

"Can I get another one?" I said.

"Sure," Anna said.

I reached under the next chicken. I felt the egg. I almost had it. Then the chicken's bony little leg twitched. That felt *weird*.

I screamed and pulled my hand out, waking up all of the chickens. They started squawking and flapping around.

I was worse than my mother.

"You dork!" Anna said, batting feathers away from her face. "Now we have to wait until they fall asleep again."

"I'm sorry! They scared me." Oh crap. I didn't want Anna to think I was a wuss.

Anna gave me a "you're hopeless" sort of look, and then she punched me in the shoulder. "City slicker."

I was pretty sure she was joking.

"Country bumpkin," I shot back, smiling.

"Let's go to the barn and see how Frida's doing," Anna said. "We'll get the eggs later."

Anna pushed the door open and sunlight poured onto the floor of the barn.

In her corner stall was huge, pregnant Frida Cowlo, chewing hay.

"Hello my beloved," Anna said. She leaned over the wall and hugged Frida. The cow nuzzled Anna's shoulder with her wet, chocolate-milk-colored nose.

A framed self-portrait by the Mexican painter Frida Kahlo hung on the barn wall next to a row of hooks. In the self-portrait, Frida Kahlo had red roses adorning her hair, gold hoop earrings in her ears, and a blue and green shawl around her shoulders. And, of course, there were her signature big black eyebrows.

"So what's with the Frida Cowlo thing?" I asked.

Anna pointed to her cow's forehead. "Check out this unibrow. It's just like Frida Kahlo's."

"Wow," I said. I hadn't noticed it before, but Frida the cow had a dark brown line above her eyes, just like Frida Kahlo's bushy, unplucked eyebrows.

"I've had her ever since she was a calf."

I didn't really understand it. We'd had beef burgers the night before for dinner, but then here was Anna, totally into her prized cow.

"What do you do with her? I mean, she can't really play fetch like a dog. Or lie on your lap like a cat."

Anna frowned at me. "Lots of things. She's way more interesting than a boring old cat."

I shrugged. Frida seemed okay as far as cows go, not that I had ever met a cow before. But it still seemed odd to have a cow as a pet.

Anna picked up a brush and started smoothing Frida's coat with it. "Isn't she silky? She won Best Jersey Cow in Show at the Interior Provincial Exhibition last year."

"Will you keep her calf when it's born?"

Anna's eyes darkened. "No. We bred Frida so that we can have her milk. We're selling her calf. We can't afford to keep two cows."

I couldn't think of anything to say to that. Anna grabbed a bucket that was beside the stall.

"I'm just going to fill this with water. Back in a second," Anna said.

I looked at Frida's face again. I had never been so close to a real cow.

She had huge, coffee-bean brown eyes with long feathery eyelashes.

Her ears flicked back and forth as she looked around her stall. Slowly, I placed my hand on her warm, strong neck and stroked it. Frida looked up at me, chewing hay, her mouth moving in small circles. This was so cool. I was making eye contact with a cow. It was like she was trying to tell me something.

At that moment I was filled with inspiration. It felt like sparkles running through my veins.

I knew exactly what to draw for the *Canvas* portrait contest.

Chapter Eight

Frida Cowlo was my ticket to New York City. I just knew it.

"Anna!" I said as she came back into the barn, lugging the now-full bucket of water. "I know who I'm going to draw for the contest!"

"Who?" she said.

I pointed to Frida with a twirly flourish of my hands.

"You think so?" Anna's jaw was set. "Why would you want to draw her for that fancy schmancy contest?"

"Well, I—," I stammered. I had no idea Anna might not go for it. "Frida is a cool-looking cow, that's why."

Anna had those narrowed eyes again. "Well," she said. "Frida and I would be honored." She scratched Frida under the chin. The cow lifted her head with her eyes closed, totally blissful.

I bet no one else was going to enter a portrait of a cow for the contest.

"Can I start now?" I could barely contain my excitement. Now that I knew what I wanted to draw, I couldn't wait to start. Anna nodded.

I rushed into the house to get my art stuff. My mom sat at the kitchen table, her back to me. She had her tarot cards spread out.

"So, you've got the Ten of Cups," my mom was saying. "This can indicate luck with money…"

Ruth looked up as I walked in. She had her apron on and flour all over her hands. She must have been in the middle of baking bread when my mom decided to give her a tarot card reading. My mom can be so inappropriate sometimes.

"Well, thank you, Lynn," Ruth said loudly. "How very…informative."

My mom looked up. "Oh, hi, Maddie. Where have you been? I've been waiting for you."

"I was just about to show your mother her job for the day," Ruth said, smiling and looking relieved.

My mom stood up and put her arm around me. "You mean *our* job for the day."

"But I was just about to—," I started to say.

"You're coming, aren't you?" Ruth said, looking wild-eyed.

My mother was pulling me toward the door. If it had just been me and mom, I would have put up a stink. But with Ruth there, I decided to tone it down.

I thought longingly of my paper and pencils. Once again, my mother was ruining *everything*. At this rate I would never get my portrait done in time.

Ruth led us to the garlic shed. I stomped along beside my mother, my arms crossed.

"What's that?" my mom asked, pointing to a small, crooked building next to the garlic shed. Some of the dirty windows were cracked. Everything else on the farm was clean, tidy and well taken care of.

"Oh, that's Anna's old playhouse," Ruth said. "Now it's full of broken tools, plant pots, that sort of thing. We haven't gotten around to doing anything with it."

My mom put her finger to her lips like she was thinking. Ruth hurried us along to the garlic shed.

"Our pride and joy," Ruth said. "Certified organic Hungarian garlic."

Bunches of garlic hung from the ceiling beams, drying on hooks. They were strung together from their stalks. I had no idea garlic grew with long stalks like that. I barely knew anything about garlic, come to think of it. My mom bought it pre-minced in a jar.

In the middle of the shed were two chairs and stacks of yellow milk crates. Each one was filled to the top with garlic bulbs. Ruth motioned for my mom and me to sit.

"You are going to help us with a big order. We need to size these bulbs," Ruth said. She held up a thin piece of wood.

It had cutouts in the shape of garlic bulbs marked *small*, *medium* and *large*.

"You measure them like so," Ruth said.

She took a bulb out of the milk crate nearest to my mom's chair. She held it up to the cutout to measure it. She then placed it in a box marked *medium*.

"That's what you do," Ruth said. "With *all* these crates of garlic."

"After this do we get to milk goats?" my mom asked. Jeez, she never gave up.

"Mom, shut *up* about the goats already," I muttered.

My mom pinched me on the back of my arm. She does that when I say something rude.

Ruth looked slightly panicked. "The goats don't need milking until, um, next week."

I stifled a laugh.

Ruth said she had to go back to her bread making. My mom picked up a garlic bulb and held it up to the cutout board, studying it for a few minutes. At this rate it would take her a week just to size one crate.

"Mom, I think we need to be a little faster than that," I said.

"Maddie, you need to cultivate patience. Repetitive work is good for the soul."

This was agony. It had to be the most boring job on the whole farm. I should have been drawing my prize-winning portrait of Frida the cow.

After my mom had measured a couple more garlic bulbs, I spotted Anna walking toward us.

"Hey, Maddie," she said. "What are you doing here? You promised to help me with my 4-H meeting now."

"The what?" I said. Anna stepped very hard on my big toe.

"Oh right," I said, finally cluing in. "The 4-H meeting!"

Anna turned to my mom. "It'll be very educational for her, Mrs. Turner. I'm so happy to have her help."

"You girls are leaving?" My mom looked disappointed. But she wanted me to learn all about tilling the earth and getting closer to the land, so she couldn't really argue.

"Here," Anna said, turning on a dirt-splattered boom box. I hadn't noticed it earlier. "You can listen to the radio."

Fuzzy country music came out of the speakers. My mom hated country music.

"But, Maddie, you'll come help me as soon as you're back from the meeting, right?" my mom said. She fiddled with the radio dial.

"It's going to be a long meeting," Anna said. "Lots on the agenda."

My mom slowly picked up a bulb. "How many of these do I need to do?"

"My dad's going to sell them at the farmer's market this weekend,"

Anna said. "So we need a lot of garlic sized." She glanced at me. "A *lot*."

I liked Anna more and more all the time.

"Okay, bye, Mom," I said.

"Bye, hon," she said with a sigh. "Have fun."

As soon as we were out of earshot, Anna said, "That should keep her busy for a while."

I may have felt a little guilty for leaving my mom with the boring garlic job. But she was the one who wanted to come here in the first place.

"So what are we doing?" I asked.

"We're going back to the barn," Anna said, "so you can start working on your prize-winning portrait of Frida."

Chapter Nine

"Can I see it?" Anna asked, poking her head around the barn door. I had been drawing for a couple of hours.

"Not yet," I replied. I don't like people to see my drawings until they have some oomph to them.

Anna nodded. She seemed to understand.

"Wouldn't it be amazing if you won the contest and we went to New York City together?" she said, keeping a respectful distance just inside the barn door.

"That would be so fun," I said, my mind swimming with ideas. "We could go to art galleries together and have lunch in delicatessens!"

"And go shopping on Fifth Avenue!" Anna said, her eyes dreamy.

"Yeah!" I said.

We both let out a squeal of excitement.

"Maybe we should go see how your mom is doing," Anna said after a few more minutes.

"At this point she's probably gone bonkers and started naming every bulb of garlic," I said.

Anna laughed. "Was your mom always like that? Into tarot cards and crystals and everything?"

"No," I said. "She used to be normal when I was a little kid. She read her horoscope, but that's about it. Now she's into psychic awareness and self-help books."

"How come?"

"I think it's because of my dad. She found out that my dad was having an affair with someone at his work. My dad has a new wife now."

"Wow," Anna said. "I can't believe your mom told you all that."

"Yeah, my mom tells me every-thing." *And most of the time I wish she didn't*, I added in my head.

"Do you miss your dad?" Anna said.

"He has two kids and a whole other life. I don't think about him much." It felt weird and a little sad telling Anna the story. "After that my mom started getting weird and New Agey," I said.

"Wow," Anna said again. "That explains a lot."

"I know." I paused. "Right now she's probably chatting away to Bob, Brenda and Biff, the Garlic Bulbs."

Anna hooted with laughter.

I was really getting into the swing of things now.

"She has a tarot-card-reading business," I said. "She goes by the name Lady Venus. She charges lots of money to desperate women looking for love. No matter which cards she gets, she says the same thing." I imitated my mom's overly dramatic Lady Venus voice. "You will meet a handsome stranger soon. Love is coming to you. Just open your heart."

Anna's jaw was hanging open. She was loving every bit of my act.

"My mom also goes to women's retreats where she and other old ladies worship the full moon and do yoga naked," I said. Dramatically, I raised my arms over my head as I'd seen my mother do.

As I was in Downward Dog pose, I looked between my legs, upside down.

My mother was standing in the shadows, right outside the barn door.

She'd heard everything.

I stood up so fast that blue and pink stars flashed in front of my eyes. Anna just stood there, her hand over her mouth, looking horrified.

I turned and ran after my mom, who was walking quickly across the yard.

"Mom!" I shouted after her. She didn't turn around.

I went back into the barn. Anna was still standing where I had left her.

"Are you in trouble?" Anna's eyes were huge. "I think she heard *everything* you said."

"Sort of," I said. I made light of it, but I felt terrible for making fun of my mom like that. "She'll give me the silent treatment for a while."

At dinner, my mom chatted loudly with Ruth and Klaus, and ignored Anna and me completely. I decided to ignore her too. It served her right.

I had bigger things to worry about. I had to finish my portrait of Frida Cowlo for the art contest.

After dinner, Anna and I hung out in her room. My mom was in the kitchen helping Ruth clean up. She was telling Ruth about the healing properties of crystals.

"Hey, so you've been borrowing my clothes all week," Anna said. "Can I try on some of yours?"

"Okay!" I said. I ran into the guest room and grabbed my duffel bag. We started going through all the clothes I'd brought.

"Cool!" Anna said, taking out my blue and white polyester dress with the big buttons.

"That's an airline stewardess uniform from the 1960s," I said. "I got it at a thrift store."

Anna pulled out a bunch of skirts and shirts to try on. She would go behind her closet door, change and strut out, model-on-the-catwalk style. I narrated the whole show.

"And here is Anna in a vintage pink poodle skirt with a bright red crinoline, plus a white Marc Jacobs shirt with a sweetheart neckline. Work it, baby!"

We were both giggling the whole time.

"It's fun with you here," Anna said, posing in a plaid short skirt, fishnets and black zippered tank top. "I don't want you to leave."

"Me neither," I said. I never thought I'd say that, but the country was way better than I expected. Especially with Anna around.

That night, after everyone was asleep, I crept out of the house with a flashlight in one hand and my drawing stuff in the other. I was itching to get back to my portrait of Frida. I had to make it the best drawing ever.

As soon as I got out to the porch, a shudder went through me. It sure got dark in the country. I shone the flashlight on the barn. It was about fifty feet away.

I took a deep breath and ran. The darkness pressed on my back in a terrifying way, like when someone chases you up the stairs. I slid the door open and leaped into the barn, sliding it closed behind me.

Frida was lying on her side in her stall, awake and breathing heavily. Her big belly must have been a lot of work to haul around. It seemed to stick out even more than it had earlier that day. She glanced up at me.

I tugged the cord to turn on the dangling light bulb beside the Frida Kahlo self-portrait on the wall. Then I pulled up a stool and got to work on my drawing. My hand started to move and sketch without me even having to think about it.

After a while I set my sketchbook down and looked at what I'd done so far. I let out a little squeal of joy. I couldn't believe how well it was turning out.

I yawned. My eyes were starting to go blurry. I could work more on the portrait the next day.

"Goodnight, Frida," I said and snapped off the light.

Chapter Ten

I had only been asleep a few minutes when a familiar voice called, "Maddie! Maddie!"

My mother was shaking my shoulder to wake me up.

"What's going on?" I said, my voice louder than I expected.

"Shhh!" My mom looked around, nervous. "We're leaving. Here's something for you to wear." She pressed a bundle of clothes into my arms.

I was way too sleepy for all this. "What are you talking about?"

As my eyes adjusted to the darkness, I saw that our bags were packed, next to the door.

"We're leaving. Now. Before those farmers wake up. This experience is not at all what I expected. I'm sick of dealing with that stupid garlic, and you're always off with Anna. Saying inappropriate things about me." Her voice was hoarse, the way it got when she was angry.

"I tried to tell you I was sorry!"

"This discussion is closed. I consulted the tarot, and I got the Queen of Wands. We're doing the right thing by leaving."

This couldn't really be happening. "Mom, we can't leave! I'm drawing Anna's cow for the art contest. I have to stay to finish it."

"We'll find some other farm with cows for you to draw." She pulled on my arm to get me out of bed.

I pushed her away. "Mom, *you* were the one who wanted to come here. I'm not leaving." I crossed my arms and stayed in bed.

My mom grabbed the bags and opened the door. I could see my sketchbook and pencils sticking out of my duffel bag.

"I'm going to the car," she said.

I jumped up and followed her. I had to get my drawing stuff back. In the hallway we ran smack into Klaus.

My mom and I gasped.

"Were you woken by the hubbub?" Klaus said, grinning. "If you want to see a calf being born, now is the time. Anna and Ruth are out in the barn with the veterinarian."

I couldn't believe it. I had just been out in the barn with Frida, and now she was giving birth.

Klaus turned to go back outside, cup of coffee in hand.

My mom whispered to me, "Now's our chance, while they're distracted. Let's go."

"If you think I'm leaving now, you're crazy," I hissed. I ran to catch up with Klaus. My mom called after me, but I didn't turn around.

As I approached the barn, I slowed down a little. Did I really want to see a calf being born?

"You coming?" Klaus asked, stepping inside.

I took a deep breath and nodded. Klaus and I tiptoed into the dimly lit barn. Anna and Ruth were standing outside Frida's stall, leaning over the wall. Anna was cooing at Frida saying, "Good girl, Frida! You can do it!"

Frida, meanwhile, was lying on her side with her legs straight out in front of her. Her sides were heaving up and down. All the while, she let out loud moos and groans. With each moo, she lifted her tail.

A man in a denim shirt and jeans was kneeling beside her, wearing a band around his head with a light attached. I guessed he was the veterinarian. His light shone right under Frida's uplifted tail.

I crept up beside Anna. Without saying a word, she put her arm around my shoulder and squeezed.

"Here it comes," the vet said.

I saw two pointy white things sticking out from under Frida's tail. I was too stunned to ask what they were.

"Those are hooves," said Ruth. It was like she read my mind.

My mom had followed me, but she stayed back. "And there's the nose!" cried Anna.

With another loud moo from Frida, a sopping wet baby cow head and two long legs emerged.

After another couple of minutes, the entire calf slid out and plopped onto the hay-covered floor. The calf was blue and covered in a white film. Frida started licking her baby with her long pink tongue.

I felt a mixture of joy and wonder. I had just seen a brand-new animal be born. This wasn't a video on YouTube. This was the real thing.

"Oh, Frida!" Anna exclaimed, running into the stall. She patted Frida's side. "I'm so proud of you."

The little brown calf strained its neck and stood up. I couldn't believe that it could stand just after being born. Anna and I hugged. Klaus smiled. Ruth snapped a few photos.

Just then, Frida let out a horrible bellow. Then another. If a cow could scream, that's what it would sound like.

The doctor frowned. He took out his stethoscope and held it under Frida's front leg. He started feeling her sides. Frida let out another scream, even louder this time.

"Frida?" Anna gasped.

The vet said something to Klaus in a low voice. He pulled out the biggest needle I'd ever seen.

"But the birth went so smoothly!" Klaus said to the vet.

What was happening? On the floor of the stall, I saw a huge pool of dark red blood.

Anna wrapped her arms around Frida's neck and started wailing. "No! Frida!"

"We must go now, Maddie." Ruth put her arm around my waist and pulled me to the door. I turned around to see Klaus holding Anna back as the vet worked on Frida.

Ruth took my mom and me outside and closed the barn door.

"Oh dear," she kept saying. "Oh dear, oh dear. Anna loves that cow so much."

"What's happening?" my mom said.

Hot tears spilled onto my cheeks. It didn't know what was going on, but it didn't look good.

"Let's go inside," Ruth said. "Not much we can do."

Ruth was too distracted to see our packed bags sitting by the door. She put the kettle on the stove for tea.

I grabbed our bags and shoved them back into our room. Then I went into the kitchen and stood at the counter with Ruth, in silence.

My mom sighed and sat at the kitchen table. After a long time and many cups of tea, we all went to bed. I couldn't sleep at all.

Chapter Eleven

I couldn't believe it. Frida Cowlo was dead.

Klaus told us at breakfast in the morning. It was something to do with a torn uterus. Ruth was in the barn, trying to comfort Anna. None of us had slept much. My eyes were blurry, and my hair was sticking out all over the place. I didn't care.

"The calf is fine," Klaus said gruffly. "But Anna is inconsolable. She stayed in the barn all night."

I set down my fork. I didn't feel like eating. Poor Frida. And poor, poor Anna.

I had a split-second thought about the contest. The deadline was in three days. Frida was supposed to be my prize-winning contest entry.

I'm a horrible, awful person, I thought.

I got up from the table. "I'm going to see Anna."

"Just a second, Maddie." My mom followed me out to the porch.

"No," I said to my mom. "You're not going to make us leave!"

"Maybe it's a good idea," she said. "They don't need us here now."

I turned and ran toward the barn. The door was closed. I knocked on it lightly.

Ruth opened the door. "Oh, come in, Maddie."

Anna was in Frida's stall. Frida was covered in a big blue blanket. One of her ears stuck out from the edge of the blanket. Anna was stroking it gently.

The little brown calf was in a stall on the other side of the barn. It was drinking milk from a huge bottle, mounted on the wall.

I didn't know what to do. I'd never had to deal with anything like this before.

"I'll miss her velvety ears so much," Anna said, still stroking. Then she covered her face with her hands and cried.

"Oh, Frida," she wailed. "My poor girl. She was so brave."

I knelt beside Anna. She didn't look up. I put my hand on her shoulder. Anna cried and cried.

Finally Ruth came over and sat next to her daughter. Anna threw her arms around Ruth's neck and kept on crying, all over Ruth's shirt.

I tiptoed out of the barn.

It was a whole different world outside. A breeze fluttered the leaves on the apple trees. Klaus was riding his tractor through one of the fields. Farm life went on as usual.

I hadn't been able to comfort Anna at all. I didn't know how to make her feel better.

Maybe my mom and I should leave, after all.

I wandered around looking for my mom. As I passed the small broken-down building beside the garlic shed, I heard some banging. I saw my mom's blond ponytail through the dirty, cracked windowpane.

"Uh, Mom?" I said, sticking my head into the crooked little doorway.

"Oh, hi, Maddie," my mom said. Her hands were full of green plastic plant pots.

"Were you still thinking about leaving?"

My mom shook her head. "Oh, no. I've got an important job to do now, you see."

I glanced around the dusty little shack. "An important job?"

My mom nodded. "I'm going to feng shui this junk shed to bring the Friesens better luck."

My mom had taken a one-day course in feng shui last fall. Ever since then, she'd been feng shui-ing everything, from our bathroom to the produce section at the grocer down the street.

"I told Klaus I could bring a better flow of *chi* to the shed. He thought it was a great idea."

Unbelievable. My mom had convinced an old farmer of the merits of an ancient Chinese interior design system. He was probably just happy to get her out of his way for a while.

My mom got back to work shuffling old pots around.

Now I really didn't know what to do with myself. I slumped into the house and went to our bedroom. I hucked myself onto the bed and lay there for a while, feeling sorry for myself.

I wanted to win that art contest so badly. It was the chance of a lifetime. But I couldn't enter the portrait now. It wouldn't be right. And it was too late to start something new.

I rolled over and pulled my sketch-book out of my bag. I turned to the portrait of Frida Cowlo.

I felt like crumpling it up in a ball or scribbling all over it with a black crayon.

But I didn't do any of those things. Instead I smoothed the edges of the page, and stared at it. I had captured Frida Cowlo's long ears, her feathery eyelashes and moist nose perfectly. I was more than halfway there.

It was a good portrait. More than good. I thought it was on its way to being great.

But it was missing something.

I crept into Anna's room and took down a photo of her and Frida. The cow had a "Best in Show" blue ribbon tied around her neck. I heard Ruth's voice in my head: *Anna loves that cow so much.*

Frida had been a big part of Anna's life.

My Frida Cowlo portrait wasn't about the *Canvas* art contest anymore. I was going to finish it for Anna.

I took the photo back to my bedroom and set it on the desk with my sketchbook and art supplies.

I sat down and picked up my black pencil with a flourish. I smiled as I drew hundreds of tiny feather strokes to create the Frida Kahlo unibrow.

Once I had finished all the fine details in pencil, I took out my pastels. I had figured out what was missing from the portrait, and I knew just what to do about it.

Chapter Twelve

By the next afternoon, the portrait was finished. I wrote my initials, *MT*, and the year in the lower right-hand corner. I held it out and gazed at it. I felt a whoosh of pride.

The cow looking out at me from the page looked exactly like Anna's beloved pet. Bright red roses adorned her head, above her dark eyebrows. Large gold hoop earrings hung from her ears. Around her shoulders was a blue and green flowered shawl just like the real Frida Kahlo's in her self-portrait. In the background I had drawn the red and white barn, the garlic shed and the river. Frida Cowlo on her farm.

I laughed to myself. I never would have guessed that my masterpiece would be a drawing of a Jersey cow. I could just imagine the magazine articles. *Early in her career, celebrated Vancouver artist Maddie Turner drew her inspiration from large farm animals.*

I was bursting to show the portrait to everyone. Closing my sketchbook, I ran out of the house. Anna and Ruth were still in the barn. My mom was still feng shui-ing the broken-down shed.

"Mom, I have to show you something!" I said, bouncing up and down.

My mom's clothes were covered in dust, and her ponytail was one giant cobweb. "Just a second, Maddie. There's too much yin over here. I need to figure out how to balance the yang with—"

I opened up my sketchbook and shoved it in her face. "Look!"

My mom set down her tools.

"Oh, Maddie," she said, her eyes going all pink in the corners. "It's…it's beautiful. Absolutely beautiful. Are you going to show it to Anna?"

I nodded. "I'm heading over to the barn right now."

"Okay," my mom said. "Wow, I've got a lot to do before we leave tomorrow. I have to fill the missing *bagua* areas here."

"Tomorrow?" I said.

"Can you believe our week on the farm is almost over?" my mom said.

So much had happened in one week.

My pace quickened as I approached the barn doors. I could hardly wait to show Anna my drawing.

But then I stopped. I had a better idea. Carefully, I placed my sketchbook on a ledge outside the barn door.

Inside, Anna was sitting in the stall nearest the door. The calf was drinking from the big bottle of milk on the wall again.

"Hi," I said, sitting down next to Anna.

"Hey," she said, petting the calf. Her eyes were red and puffy from crying. "I'm going to name her Frida Junior. Look."

She turned the calf's face toward me. Frida Junior had the same dark eyebrow markings as her mother.

"My dad said I can keep her," Anna said. "She's sweet, but I just want Frida back."

Then she started crying all over again. It made me cry too. We sat together petting Frida Junior, our tears falling on her silky fur.

The next morning, my mother decided it was time for her big reveal. She assembled Ruth, Klaus and me in front of the junk shed she'd been working on. She'd asked us to keep our eyes closed from the porch to the shack.

"Ta-da!" she said, flinging her arms above her head. "The junk shed has been officially feng shui-ed. The yin and the yang are in balance."

My mom looked proud. Ruth, Klaus and I squished around the door and looked in. Ruth looked hopeful at first. Then her face fell.

Inside the shed, stacks of cracked plant pots stretched from floor to ceiling. There must have been about eight stacks, all crammed on one side of the shed. Take one pot off the stack, and the whole thing would fall over. In the middle of the shed was a big pot full of water, with a few rose blossoms floating in it. I recognized the roses from Ruth's well-tended rosebush in the front yard.

"That's your water feature," said my mom. "Very important. You need to change that water every two days, or else it'll go stagnant."

The Friesens, of course, were too polite to say anything. But I saw them exchange looks that said, *We'll have to fix this when she leaves*.

"Uh, well, thank you, Lynn," Ruth said. "For all your hard work."

"I am glad to provide my helping hands where needed," my mom said, "and to teach you a little about feng shui along the way."

She didn't get it. These nice farmers couldn't wait to get rid of her, and she thought she'd done them a great service. I had that familiar I-could-just-die feeling again.

Smiling, my mother turned to me.

"All packed, Maddie?" she asked.

"All packed," I replied.

"Okay," she said. "See you at the car."

"I just need to do one last thing," I said.

I hurried to the guest bedroom and opened the big drawer in the desk. There it sat, my portrait of Frida Cowlo. My masterpiece. I had wrapped it up in two blank pages from my sketchbook. I thought about looking at it one last time, but I decided not to. It might break my heart.

I leaned the wrapped-up portrait against Anna's bedroom door.

I turned and walked away. At the end of the hall, I hesitated. *You're doing it for Anna,* I reminded myself, *and Frida.*

I walked out into the hot summer morning, leaving my chances at winning the *Canvas* art contest behind.

The Friesens were gathered around my mom's car. By some miracle, she was able to start it after all that sputtering on our way there.

"Thank you for coming," Ruth said, clasping my hands and then my mother's hands.

"It has been interesting," said Klaus, winking at me.

Anna had come out of the barn to say goodbye. She gave me a big hug.

"Bye, Maddie. I'm really going to miss you." Her voice came out whispery. She seemed too worn-out to say much more than that.

"I'll miss you too," I said.

I hate goodbyes. They're the worst. I hopped in the car before I started blubbering. Or worse, before I decided to run back in the house for the portrait of Frida Cowlo.

I waved as we drove down the long dusty driveway. The Friesens waved back.

There were a few blissful moments in the car when my mother didn't speak.

When I say a few moments, I mean a grand total of about twenty-seven seconds.

"Well, that was fun. I'm so glad I could be of service to the Friesens."

I didn't say anything.

"It was a lot of work reorganizing that shed," my mom continued. "But in the end I really improved the flow of *chi*."

I couldn't hold it in anymore. My chest felt heavy, and I burst into tears.

"What's the matter, Madison?" my mom said, her eyebrows knitted together.

I still didn't say anything. I couldn't, with all the tears and the hefty helping of snot.

"Are you sad about leaving the farm?" she said.

"I guess so," I said.

I was crying for Anna, and Frida, and the little calf without a mother. And I was crying because I left my beautiful, possibly prize-winning portrait behind. I am such an idiot, I kept thinking. Now I'll never get to New York City. That was my big chance.

"See," she said, sounding pleased with herself. "I told you that city girls can learn to love the country."

I balled my hands up into fists. I wanted to scream at my mother to turn the car around so that I could get my drawing back. Instead I looked out the window as the perfect green rows of vegetables whipped by.

Bit by bit, I felt my hands relax. I wondered if Anna had discovered the portrait yet.

"So, for next summer's adventure," my mom was saying, "there's this nice little ashram in the Kootenays. You can do yoga up to six times a day if you want to. A girlfriend of mine went there a couple of years ago and loved it."

My mom went on and on. I closed my eyes behind my sunglasses and fell asleep.

Chapter Thirteen

Life got back to normal when my mom and I returned home to the city. My mom put her pantyhose on and went to work. I returned to my life as a teenager in the summertime, which meant hanging around the house and watching old movies all day. I did some baby-sitting, and I hung out with my friends. I went to the art gallery and worked on my *Downtown Soles* drawings. My latest drawing was a pair of red high heels against a graffiti-covered alley wall. Life felt different though. I didn't have the hopes of the New York City trip and the cover of *Canvas Magazine* to look forward to. A week after we got back from the farm, I got a card in the mail from Anna. *Thank You*, it said in fancy scrollwork letters on the front. *Thank you for the incredible portrait, Maddie!* Anna had written on the inside of the card. *I can't believe you gave it to me. You're the best. Love, Anna.* My heart thumped with pride. It also broke a little. I sometimes couldn't believe I had given her the portrait either. But I was glad I had.

Anna and I had been chatting online and emailing almost every day since I got her thank-you card. She sent me updates and photos of Frida Junior.

The long, hot days and weeks went by, and soon it was the last week of

August. School was going to start again soon.

On the Friday before the first day of school, I got a brown envelope in the mail. *Canvas Magazine*, it said on the front of the envelope. It was always fun getting my magazine in the mail. But now it was a little sad too.

I ripped open the envelope. I might as well see who had won the contest.

I pulled out the September issue of *Canvas*. It had a typed letter paperclipped to the front cover. Weird, I thought. The magazine didn't usually come with a letter.

Dear Madison, the letter said. *Thank you for your entry, "Frida Cowlo," for our "Face of Youth" Art Contest. We are pleased to announce that you are First Runner-up.*

Holy. Crap. Was this a dream? I read the first part of the letter over and over.

How did my picture get entered in the contest? Finally I decided to read on.

Your prize includes $500 cash and an all-access pass to New York City's major art galleries. We hope that you will enjoy your full-page portrait, printed on page thirty-six of the enclosed September issue. Thank you for your excellent entry.

I let out a big, loud, whooping scream of surprise and happiness. I danced around the apartment, clutching the letter over my head. I plopped myself on the floor and rolled around with giddiness. I read the letter about twenty times.

I flipped to page thirty-six. I screamed all over again. There was Frida Cowlo in all her colorful glory. At the bottom of the page it said: *Frida Cowlo, by Madison Turner, age fifteen, Vancouver, BC, Canada.* I pinched myself. This wasn't a dream.

I was so glad to have a copy of the portrait. It really was the best piece I had ever drawn. It was probably the best piece I would *ever* draw.

I flipped to the cover of the magazine, to the winning portrait. It was an intricate line drawing of an old woman's face, with heavily wrinkled eyes and a small, sad-looking smile. *"Face of Youth" Art Contest Winner—Grandma Violet, by Jessie Sayers, age fourteen, Portland, ME*, it said. The artist had gotten the light and shading on the old woman's face just right. It was an excellent portrait.

Then I tried to analyze how it had all happened. Anna would have known that the contest deadline was coming up. She must have figured out where and how to send it. Wow. This was too much to take in.

I leaped up and ran to the phone. I dialed the Friesens' number. Anna answered.

I didn't even say hello. "I'm First Runner-up!" I blurted.

"You didn't win?" Anna said. "That's ridiculous!"

"But, Anna, how did you—? Where did you—? I can't believe you entered my portrait in the contest!" I said.

"The Internet is a wonderful thing," Anna said in her matter-of-fact tone. "I looked up the *Canvas Magazine* website, found the contest details, went to town and mailed it. My parents had your address from your mom's volunteer application."

Anna made the amazing thing that she had done sound so straightforward.

"But you sent the portrait in to the contest?" I implored. "The whole idea was for you to keep it!"

"Ever hear of digital copies?" Anna said. "I mailed a copy to the contest. I kept the original."

Oh right. Duh. I hadn't thought of that.

"How did you keep it from me all this time?" I said.

Anna laughed. "I'm pretty good at keeping a secret. So, what's your prize?"

"Five hundred dollars in cash, a pass to New York City's art galleries, and the portrait is in the magazine," I said.

"You can get tickets to fly to New York for only six hundred, on a good deal! You'll just have to save a little more," Anna said, sounding excited. "We can go together next summer. We can stay with my brother, Thomas. We might have to sleep in his bathtub, but that's okay!"

Anna was right. We could still go to New York City, even if I hadn't won first prize.

"Yes," I said. "Yes, yes, yes!"

I started jumping up and down as I said it. After Anna and I talked about our Manhattan plans for a while, I hung up.

I couldn't wait to go on my dream trip to New York. No tarot cards. No Reiki. No feng shui. This was going to be *my* adventure.

Acknowledgments

A very big thank-you to my wonderful editor, Melanie Jeffs, for your thoughtful, perceptive comments and changes.

To Heather Bell, Janis McKenzie, Pat Maher, Zoë Howard, Laura Dodwell-Groves and the Inkslingers—Rachelle Delaney, Lori Sherritt, Tanya Kyi, Maryn Quarless and Kallie George—many thanks for your friendship, feedback and support.

Much love and gratitude, as always, to my amazing Joshua and my family.